Jeanie & Genie

WHEN WISHES GO WRONG

BY **TRISH GRANTED**
ILLUSTRATED BY **MANUELA LÓPEZ**

LIT
New York   London

This book is a work of fiction. Any references to historical events, real people, or real places are used fictitiously. Other names, characters, places, and events are products of the author's imagination, and any resemblance to actual events or places or persons, living or dead, is entirely coincidental.

LITTLE SIMON

An imprint of Simon & Schuster Children's Publishing Division · 1230 Avenue of the Americas, New York, New York 10020 · First Little Simon hardcover edition November 2021

Copyright © 2021 by Simon & Schuster, Inc.

All rights reserved, including the right of reproduction in whole or in part in any form.

LITTLE SIMON is a registered trademark of Simon & Schuster, Inc., and associated colophon is a trademark of Simon & Schuster, Inc.

For information about special discounts for bulk purchases, please contact Simon & Schuster Special Sales at 1-866-506-1949 or business@simonandschuster.com.

The Simon & Schuster Speakers Bureau can bring authors to your live event. For more information or to book an event contact the Simon & Schuster Speakers Bureau at 1-866-248-3049 or visit our website at www.simonspeakers.com.

Designed by Brittany Fetcho

Manufactured in the United States of America 1021 FFG

10 9 8 7 6 5 4 3 2 1

Library of Congress Cataloging-in-Publication Data

Names: Granted, Trish, author. | López, Manuela, 1985- illustrator. Title: When wishes go wrong / by Trish Granted ; illustrated by Manuela López. Description: First Little Simon paperback edition. | New York : Little Simon, 2021. | Series: Jeanie & genie ; 6 | Audience: Ages 5-9. | Summary: A lunar eclipse has unexpected consequences for Willow's wish granting magic, causing big problems for Jeanie and Willow. Identifiers: LCCN 2021017785 (print) | LCCN 2021017786 (ebook) | ISBN 9781534487024 (pbk) | ISBN 9781534487031 (hc) | ISBN 9781534487048 (ebook) Subjects: CYAC: Wishes—Fiction. | Genies—Fiction. | Magic—Fiction. | Lunar eclipses—Fiction. | LCGFT: Novels. Classification: LCC PZ7.1.G728 Wh 2021 (print) | LCC PZ7.1.G728 (ebook) | DDC [Fic]—dc23 LC record available at https://lccn.loc.gov/2021017785 LC ebook record available at https://lccn.loc.gov/2021017786

TABLE OF CONTENTS

TOP SECRET BUSINESS

"Star light, star bright, first star I see to—"

"Oh no you don't!" said Jeanie Bell. She folded down the corner of a page in her language arts workbook. Then she hopped off her bed and joined her best friend, Willow Davis, by the bedroom window. "No wishes tonight. We still have to finish our homework."

It was a school night, and just because Jeanie and Willow were having a sleepover, that was no excuse to skip out on work.

Normally Jeanie would never agree to a sleepover during the week. She couldn't have such distractions while doing her homework! But Willow's mother was away on a last-minute business trip. So Jeanie—and her parents—had agreed that Willow should stay at the Bells' house.

"I mean it, Willow," said Jeanie. "No wishes."

"No wishes," Willow promised.

"It's just . . . the sky looks so pretty with the sun setting and the stars coming out. Don't you want to say hello?"

"Um, I guess so," Jeanie said. She didn't usually talk to anything that couldn't talk back. But when she hung out with Willow, she found herself doing all sorts of unusual things.

"I've always wanted to make friends with the stars. They're so . . . twinkly," Willow mused. "I wonder if my mom is gazing up at this very same sky right now."

"Isn't she busy working?" Jeanie wondered.

Willow hesitated. "Well . . . yes, but . . . it's complicated."

Jeanie's eyes narrowed. "What sort of business trip is this, anyway?" she asked.

"Top secret business," Willow replied.

Jeanie crossed her arms, waiting for Willow to spill the beans.

Willow smiled. "Okay, do you promise not to tell anyone?"

"Have I told anyone *your* top secret?" Jeanie reminded Willow.

Sometimes Jeanie still found it hard to believe that Willow was a genie. But she'd seen Willow grant wishes with her very own eyes. And although it was a shock at first, having a genie for a best friend could be pretty cool—especially when you wanted to have pizza for dinner or get out of playing dodgeball.

The World Genie Association handbook said Willow could only tell one person her secret. And Willow had chosen Jeanie. If anyone else found out, Willow would never become a Master Genie. And that's what Willow had spent her life training for! Jeanie certainly wasn't going to give away the secret and ruin Willow's chances.

"Okay, here it is," said Willow. "There's going to be a total lunar eclipse tonight."

Jeanie considered this. She knew that Willow's mom had lots of star charts on her office walls. But what did the eclipse have to do with her work as head of the World Genie Association?

Willow continued. "During an eclipse, stars can get misaligned, comets can veer off course—the whole galaxy can tilt out of whack! So my mom had to go to headquarters to make sure everything is under control . . . cosmically speaking, of course."

Jeanie still didn't quite understand. But she'd always wanted to see an eclipse.

"We should have a viewing party," she decided. "We'll need to gather supplies and set up for optimal observation. But first . . ." Jeanie glanced at her workbook.

Willow followed Jeanie's gaze.

"I know, I know," Willow said with a laugh. "First, we finish our homework!"

Chapter 2

JUST YOUR AVERAGE ECLIPSE

Willow was amazed at how quickly Jeanie got her whole family excited to watch the eclipse.

But she wasn't surprised. When Jeanie put her mind to something, she gave 110 percent. And right now, all that brainpower was focused on the viewing party.

Jeanie had piled up a bunch of pillows on the front porch. She'd instructed her mom to find her birding binoculars, and her dad had offered to bake black-and-white *eclipse* cookies. Even Jeanie's brother, Jake, was excited. He was going to draw a picture of the eclipse for show-and-tell tomorrow.

"I just need to rub a black crayon all across my paper," he told Willow as they both collected supplies from the living room. "Easiest picture ever." Jake rifled through the arts-and-crafts drawer while Willow grabbed some blankets from the living room to bring outside.

"True," said Willow. "But there's so much more to an eclipse than just the disappearing moon. An eclipse changes the energy of the whole universe. It's like the sky is winking at you."

"I can wink too," Jake said as he tried—and failed—to shut only one eye. "See?"

Willow laughed. But she couldn't help feeling the teensiest bit nervous, too. Eclipses weren't *all* fun and games. They could be unpredictable—even more unpredictable than Willow's own wish-granting skills. Willow was a genie *in training*, so things didn't always go according to plan.

When Willow's mom had dropped her off for the sleepover earlier that day, she had seemed nervous. And she rarely seemed nervous. Willow noticed that her aura—the energy around her—was off too.  It was a swirly, stormy gray. And the crystal that hung from the rearview mirror had been swinging all over the place! But Willow knew her mom could handle whatever might happen.

"Willow!" Jeanie hollered. "You're going to miss it!"

"Coming!" Willow called.

She followed Jake outside, grabbed a cookie, and plopped down on some pillows. Then she wrapped a fuzzy blanket around herself.

By now the sky was a sea of stars. Then, very slowly, a shadow began to creep across the moon. The moon gave off a red glow that lit the black-velvet night. While Willow watched the eclipse, the world seemed totally still. Then, slowly, the shadow crept away.

Jeanie set down her binoculars. "Well, that was just as cool as I'd hoped it would be!" she said excitedly.

Willow nodded. It may have been just as cool as Jeanie had hoped it would be, but it was just as *uncool* and totally average as Willow had hoped it would be.

What was I so worried about anyway? An energy whirlpool? A comet collision? Willow couldn't help but laugh at herself.

But as they cleaned up and headed inside, Willow suddenly felt a prickly, electric feeling across the back of her neck. And the lamp charm she always wore around her neck was warm.

Willow's heart raced. She usually only felt those things when she'd granted a wish.

But she hadn't granted a wish . . . right?

Chapter 3

A TALKING DOG?

The girls were ready for bed: Pajamas were on, teeth were brushed, and lights were out.

But Jeanie was too excited to sleep. She kept thinking about the eclipse.

"Now I want glow-in-the-dark star stickers," she said to Willow. "And we could make a totally accurate map of the galaxy on my ceiling. Maybe

27

even with an eclipsed moon! What do you think?"

Willow was silent. That was odd because Willow *never* fell asleep first. She usually chattered on about dreams and rainbows and ladybugs long after Jeanie had dozed off.

"Psst! Willow, are you awake?"

"What? Oh yeah . . . ," mumbled Willow.

Jeanie sat up in bed. "What's going on with you?"

Willow hugged Mr. Whiskers tightly. "It's just . . . something weird happened right after the eclipse. I felt that prickly feeling. And my lamp charm was warm. What if I accidentally—"

"No way," Jeanie interrupted. "No one wished for anything. And if they didn't say it, you didn't do it. That's just simple cause and effect."

"You're sure?" Willow asked.

"I'm sure. If you'd done any magic, we would have seen it. There would be proof."

"Right! Proof!" said Willow. "Do you ever wonder if anyone can prove that the blue sky I see is the same color blue as the one you see and what actually sits at the end of a rainbow or . . ."

Jeanie smiled. *That's the Willow I know,* she thought as she drifted off to sleep.

When Jeanie woke up the next morning, the first thing she thought of was the eclipse from the night before. The next thing she thought of was Willow's worry that she'd granted some sort of wish. But as Jeanie looked around, she was even more sure about what she'd told Willow: No wish had been granted. The sun had come out. Jake was singing in the bathroom. Mr. Whiskers hadn't suddenly come to life. Everything was totally normal.

"Even breakfast is normal," Jeanie said as she plopped down at the kitchen table. "Our cereal is *usually* a little mushy."

"Yup," agreed Willow. "And Bear wants something, like always." Jeanie's dog wound between their legs, barking up a storm.

Just then, Jeanie's mom rushed through the kitchen, briefcase in hand.

"Hi, girls! I'm running late," she said, grabbing a banana. "Dad will take you to school today."

"Arf! Arf!" Bear barked and followed her to the door.

"Jeanie, did you feed Bear this morning?" Jeanie's mom asked between the dog's loud barks.

"Yup," said Jeanie. "I filled his water bowl too."

Jeanie's mom sighed. "Oh, Bear. Sometimes I wish you could just tell us what you want!"

Bear nuzzled the doorknob and barked again.

"*Out!*"

Jeanie froze. Had Bear just said . . . "out"?

She glanced at Willow and mouthed, *Did you hear that?*

Willow nodded.

Maybe things weren't as normal as Jeanie had thought.

Chapter 4

SURPRISE, SURPRISE!

Willow didn't say a word on the car ride to school. She didn't want to accidentally make the car fly or do anything that would grant even the smallest wish. Jeanie was silent too, and Willow knew she was thinking the same thing.

"Everything okay?" Mr. Bell asked the girls.

They both nodded. But Willow

knew deep down inside that everything was *not* okay. The prickle on the back of her neck told her so.

When the car finally pulled to the front of the carpool line, Willow and Jeanie hopped out.

The minute they were alone, Willow started talking so fast, she barely had time to breathe.

Jeanie nodded. "Well, I guess it's good that she was running too late to notice anything," she said. "And that we took Bear out right away."

"What if he'd said 'banana' next?" Willow worried as they walked down the hallway. "Your mom would have flipped."

"Your dog talked this mor<!--cut-->
But . . . but . . . when your mom wis<!--cut-->
for that, she wasn't looking m<!--cut-->
the eye. And the WGA handb<!--cut-->
says that eye contact is required<!--cut-->
wish granting . . . and what if y<!--cut-->
mom heard what Bear said?" Wil<!--cut-->
gasped, finally coming up for air.

Jeanie glanced up at the hall clock. "Come on. There's no point being worried *and* late."

Willow managed a smile. She appreciated that Jeanie was trying to remain calm. Usually it was the other way around, with *Willow* calming *Jeanie* down.

In the classroom, Willow went to put her backpack away. Zora Klein and Nico Romero were doing the same. Zora's backpack landed with a thud.

"That thing is so heavy!" Zora complained as they all headed for their desks.

"Maybe Jelly Bean will help you carry it home this afternoon," Nico joked.

That made Willow giggle. Jelly Bean was their class hamster, and she couldn't imagine him lifting the giant bag with his tiny furry paws.

"Seriously, don't you wish our bags could fly or something?" Zora said.

But Willow stopped laughing. Behind Zora and Nico, she saw something strange happening outside the classroom window.

A dozen winged backpacks were flying around the playground!

"Um, Willow, are you seeing what I'm seeing?" Jeanie whispered.

Willow nodded.

"Good morning, class," said Ms. Patel from the front of the room. "Take out your language arts workbooks, please."

"I don't care about lugging my backpack around," Nico said to Zora as he opened his book. "But I do wish I didn't have to practice my cello."

Just then, the sound of a symphony filled the classroom. Everyone stopped what they were doing to listen.

Willow's jaw dropped open.

Then, just as suddenly as the music started, it stopped.

"Well, that was a lovely surprise," said Ms. Patel. "Sounds like you're all in for a treat during your music class this afternoon."

Willow buried her head in her hands. It may have been a surprise, but it was not exactly a lovely one. Not for Willow.

MIXED-UP MAGIC

Two more minutes, Jeanie thought as she watched the second hand tick slowly around the clock above Ms. Patel's desk.

Jeanie had never wanted class to end so badly before. She loved learning. But if her classmates kept making wishes, someone was going to notice the strange things happening around Rivertown Elementary today.

She and Willow had to come up with a plan during recess.

Tick, tick, tick . . . RING!

Finally! Jeanie grabbed Willow's hand and hurried her out the door. But not before she heard Finn Crowley's tummy rumble.

Finn's cheeks went red. "I wish we had lunch now, instead of recess," he said.

Jeanie froze and closed her eyes. *I wish.* Those two little words made *her* tummy rumble . . . with worry!

As the rest of the class filed out of the room, Jeanie took a deep breath. "Willow, I think we need to—"

"Look out!" Willow pushed Jeanie toward the chalkboard just as a giant meatball and hundreds of spaghetti strands fell out of the air. They'd been seconds away from a spaghetti-and-meatball disaster!

"What. Was. That?" Jeanie said staring at the mess on the floor.

Willow shook her head. "Lunch?"

"We've got to get rid of this food before anyone sees," said Jeanie. "Can you do that, Willow?"

Willow thought for a moment. "Maybe! The mess-be-gone spell should do the trick!" She closed her eyes.

"Mess be gone," she began, then stopped. "Mess, mess, go away," she tried again, then stopped again.

Jeanie was starting to get worried. Would Willow be able to remember the spell?

"This mess must go, my charm will glow, clean up like whoa, go fast not slow!"

Jeanie closed her eyes, afraid to look. Then she heard a loud *poof!* When she slowly opened her eyes, the spaghetti and meatballs were gone. Phew!

Outside, the playground was a zoo. Literally! When Max Mercado mentioned that he wished his project on the *Milky* Way was almost done, a cow suddenly appeared on the soccer field. Jeanie dodged in front of it while Willow used the invisi-bull charm so no one could see it. Luckily, it worked.

Then Jeanie overheard Emily Craig talk about a purple headband she wished she had worn today since it was so windy, and suddenly Emily's hair *itself* turned purple. Willow quickly zapped it back to its usual brown before anyone noticed.

By the end of recess, Jeanie was exhausted. She wasn't sure how much more of this mixed-up magic she could take!

BAD NEWS

That afternoon, Willow watched Jeanie fidget and pace in the carpool line. Willow thought about all that had happened that day.

When the bulletin board letters started floating during the spelling test, Jeanie had distracted everyone by acting like she'd seen something out the window. Then Willow had commanded the letters to return to their positions. And when everyone had accidentally fallen asleep during their math lesson, Jeanie had helped Willow remember that there was a sleep-no-more spell she could use to wake them up.

"No one noticed anything strange today," Willow said to Jeanie. "At least, I don't *think* they did."

Jeanie nodded, though Willow could tell she was still feeling nervous.

This is all my fault, Willow thought. *If I hadn't come to Rivertown, my wish granting wouldn't be going so . . . wrong. And my best friend wouldn't be so stressed trying to hide it all.*

Luckily, Willow's mom would be there any minute to pick her up. Willow sure hoped she'd know how to make everything right again.

For the time being, Willow closed her eyes, took a deep breath, and pictured a rainbow waterfall rushing over a crystal mountain . . . her happy place.

BEEP! BEEP! Jeanie's dad honked as he pulled his car to the front of the line.

"Good news, girls!" he called. "You get to have another sleepover tonight!"

"That's . . . um . . . great, Mr. Bell," Willow stammered. "But my mom's going to be here soon and—"

Mr. Bell shook his head. "She called. Her business is taking longer than she planned, so she asked if you could stay at our house again tonight."

Willow's heart sank. Normally she loved sleepovers at Jeanie's house. And two in a row meant they could  do everything they hadn't had time for the night before: splatter-paint their jeans with glittery colors, practice cartwheels in the backyard, and build the biggest pillow fort ever.

But Willow didn't want to do any of those things today. Suddenly *she* was the one who felt like a ball of nerves.

Willow pulled on Jeanie's sleeve. "Without my mom, I don't know how to stop granting all these accidental wishes."

CAT-ASTROPHE!

"Okay, we need to attack this problem logically," Jeanie said when the girls got home. "First, we shouldn't go near anyone who might say anything even close to 'I wish.'"

"Even Jake?" asked Willow.

"Especially Jake."

They'd stopped in the kitchen for a snack, but when Jake came barreling in yelling about how he wanted to play with his race cars and needed more of those eclipse cookies, Jeanie whisked Willow up to her bedroom and locked the door.

"Second, we need to figure
out how these wishes work," she
continued. "If no one's looking you in
the eye and asking directly, how are
you granting anything?"

"I don't know," said Willow. "Maybe it's—wait, do you hear that?"

Outside, someone was laughing and shouting delightedly. Actually, it wasn't just one person. It was a *lot* of people.

The girls rushed to the window. Every kid in the neighborhood was across the street, madly scooping up piles of chocolate bars, candy necklaces, and lollipops that were sprinkled around the yard.

"It looks like the world's biggest piñata exploded over there," said Willow. "Someone must have wished for a sweet treat."

Jeanie's neighbor, Mr. Penny, tried to shoo the kids away from his prize-winning rosebushes, but the candy grab was way too good for anyone to pass up.

Jeanie couldn't believe what she was seeing. "This doesn't make any sense. How can you have granted a wish you didn't even hear? This is turning into a total catastrophe!"

Jeanie felt a sudden tingle on her scalp. That was strange.

"Um . . . Jeanie," Willow said, her eyes as big as flying saucers. "I think you better look in the mirror."

Jeanie ran over to the one hanging on her closet door. Were those . . . cat ears?

"I guess you shouldn't have said *cat*-astrophe . . . ," said Willow, clearly trying *not* to smile.

"Very funny. Can you do something about this?" Jeanie asked waving her hands around her head. "Before I sprout whiskers, too?"

Willow recited the words to the meow-or-later charm, and—*poof!*—the cat ears were gone.

Jeanie let out a big breath she hadn't realized she'd been holding.

"What are we going to do about all this . . . chaos?"

Willow thought for a moment. "Well, we may not know why wishes are being granted. But we are expert distractors. We just need a plan to keep covering them up until my mom gets back."

A plan? Lucky for Willow, planning was Jeanie's specialty.

Chapter 8

AN UNEXPECTED VISITOR

The next morning, Willow woke up feeling lighter than a feather floating in the breeze.

She and Jeanie had spent the previous evening going over all the ways they could continue to keep Willow's secret.

Willow had practiced every disappearing charm she knew—twice. She'd had a little trouble remembering the words to the fly-away spell, which meant that at one point Jeanie's desk actually lifted into the air. But as Jeanie always said, *Practice makes perfect!*

Then the girls had run some drills to quicken their reflexes. They'd rehearsed jumping in front of suspicious objects—Jeanie's bed made a good landing pad. They'd improvised stories—Willow was a natural. She had a knack for making up tales! And they'd practiced creating distractions—singing as loudly and as off-key as possible always seemed to work.

And that was why Willow was feeling a whole lot more confident.

"I have to admit," Willow said as the girls got dressed, "I usually like to go wherever the wind takes me. But right now, having a plan makes me *way* less worried."

Jeanie nodded in agreement.

"Now at least we'll be *prepared* for whatever surprises come our way."

But as the girls headed downstairs for breakfast, Willow was not prepared for the surprise that awaited her.

"Mom!" she cried. There was her mother, standing in the Bells' kitchen! Willow rushed over and gave her a big hug.

"Hi, sweetie!" Mrs. Davis said. "I got back early, so I thought I'd stop by and take you girls to school. I missed you so much!"

"I missed you, too, Mom," gushed Willow. "You have no idea *how* much!"

Then Mr. Bell brought a platter of eggs and bacon to the table. "Who's hungry?" he asked.

"Arf!" Bear barked.

"Bear's *always* hungry," Jake said.

Willow waited for Bear to say something more, but he only barked again. A regular old dog bark. Willow breathed a sigh of relief. If Bear was back to normal, maybe there was hope for her, too!

THAT EXPLAINS IT!

Breakfast that morning felt like a party. Everyone talked and laughed and ate.

And the best part, Jeanie thought, *is that Willow's mom is back!*

The minute she'd seen Mrs. Davis sitting at the table, relief had washed over her. And now that she and Willow were piling into Mrs. Davis's

car, Jeanie hoped they'd finally
have some help getting things under
control.

As soon as their seat belts clicked
into place, Jeanie shot Willow a look
and nodded toward her mother.

"Um, Mom . . . I've got to tell you something," Willow began. "Something is going seriously wrong with my wish granting."

"I know," said Mrs. Davis.

Jeanie couldn't believe her ears! She knew Willow's mom was in charge of the World Genie Association, but could she also read minds?

"It's the eclipse," Mrs. Davis explained. "The cosmic energy it created has caused all sorts of trouble. I knew it was a possibility, which is why I've had to spend so much time at WGA headquarters monitoring the situation. I had no idea how difficult this celestial event was going to be."

"What happened?" Jeanie couldn't help asking.

"Oh, it was different for everyone. It caused some genies to grant the opposite of every wish that was asked of them," Mrs. Davis replied. "Others lost their wish-granting powers entirely. And for some, just having the words 'I wish' spoken anywhere near them meant their magic was activated . . . whether they were trying to do it or not."

"That's what happened to me!" cried Willow.

Mrs. Davis gave her a reassuring smile. "Fortunately, we keep very good records at the WGA. And we know that there is going to be a shooting star tonight."

"Will that fix the ... cosmic energy or whatever?" Jeanie asked.

Mrs. Davis nodded. "But, Willow, you'll still have to be careful at school today. Remember, try not to go near anyone who might be wishing for anything."

"I'll do my best," said Willow.

Jeanie smiled. "Don't worry, Mrs. Bell. We've been practicing for this. . . ."

From the moment the morning bell rang until class was dismissed, Jeanie made sure no one talked to Willow at all.

When Ms. Patel called for volunteers during their science lesson, Jeanie jumped in front of Willow and waved her hand in the air to be picked.

During recess, she and Willow hid from their friends under the big oak tree.

And when the class split into groups to talk about the story they were reading for language arts, Jeanie elbowed Willow in the side.

"Don't you have to go to the bathroom?" she whispered to Willow.

"Oh. Um . . . yes," Willow whispered back. "Yes, I do."

In fact, Willow found lots of reasons to leave the classroom. Sip from the water fountain? Check. Visit to the nurse's office for a headache? Check. Another bathroom break? Check.

And each time Willow left, Jeanie found a way to draw attention to herself instead. She asked lots of questions. She volunteered lots of answers. She even cracked a few jokes.

It wasn't easy, but somehow Jeanie and Willow made it through the whole day without a problem.

I can't wait for the shooting star tonight, Jeanie thought to herself. *I just wish—nope! I don't wish anything! At least . . . not until tomorrow.*

Chapter 10

STAR O'CLOCK

"It's almost time!" Willow shouted as she ran into the kitchen that night, her socks sliding across the tiled floor. "Can we make popcorn?"

"Already on it," Willow's mom said, pointing to the big bowl on the counter.

Willow pulled a bag of kernels from the pantry. She was about to put it in the microwave when her mom stopped her.

"I said I'm on it." She winked at Willow, then turned her gaze to the popcorn.

ZAP!

Willow giggled. Instant popcorn was even more instant in the Davis house. She couldn't wait to learn that zapping spell!

She emptied the bag into the bowl and followed her mother upstairs. The window in Willow's room had a perfect view of the moon. While she pulled beanbag chairs over to it, her mom lit some candles.

"I'm so glad you're back," Willow said to her mom for probably the twentieth time.

"Me too, sweetie," said Mrs. Davis. "But you handled everything wonderfully."

"Thanks," said Willow. "But I'd never have gotten through the last two days without Jeanie. Especially the way she helped me practice making all those strange things disappear. I've gotten *way* better at that!"

Suddenly the sound of wind chimes filled the air.

That's funny, thought Willow. *The window's not even open!*

Then a small, sparkling cloud appeared over Willow's head, and a tiny golden box floated down, right into her hands. Inside Willow found a badge embroidered with a cute little ghost in silver thread.

"It's your Making Unwanted Things Disappear badge," her mom gushed. "I'm so proud of you, honey!"

Just then a star went zooming across the sky.

"It's happening!" cried Willow. For a moment, the world felt still, just like it had during the eclipse.

And then Willow felt an electric prickle on the back of her neck. Soon her lamp charm grew warm to the touch.

"That should do the trick," said Willow's mom. "But just to be sure, I'm going to go update my star charts and make sure there aren't any more cosmic disturbances on the way."

She ran to her office but was back moments later. "We're all set!"

Willow was so happy, she felt she might be glowing as bright as the moon. She'd earned another genie skill badge, *and* her wish granting was back to normal. Well . . . as normal as it could be for a genie who still had a lot to learn!